go ahead. Take a peek.

You know you want to...

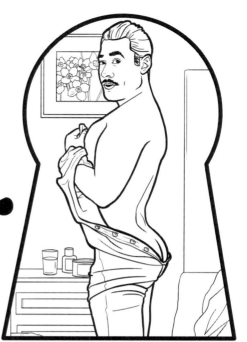

I started painting Cheesecake Boys because I was always fascinated with pinup art from the 40's and 50's. It was a more innocent time (at least on the surface), and I love the elaborate scenarios that artists like Gil Elvgren and Art Frahm concocted in order to justify disrobing their subjects. It struck me that male models were never portrayed in the same way. While it was considered sexy for a woman's skirt to be ripped off before a crowd of oglers, male pinups of that era (beefcakes) were generally only exposed by choice.

Times certainly have changed! Guys may have had a free pass on wardrobe malfunctions in the good old days, but now the Cheesecake Boys are here to even the score! I hope you have as much fun coloring this collection of pinup boys as I had drawing them. I'd love to see your creations. If you feel like showing it off as much as these fellas, post pics of your work to social media with the hashtag #PAULRICHMONDSTUDIO so I can check it out.

happy coloring!

Paul

Published by
DREAMSPINNER PRESS

5032 Capital Circle SW, Suite 2, PMB# 279, Tallahassee, FL 32305-7886 USA
www.dreamspinnerpress.com

Models for Interior Art:
Alan Ilagan, alanilagan.com.
Chris Bryant, @tenderchris (Instagram).
Tyler Wallach, tylerwallachstudio.com.

ISBN: 978-1-63533-741-9
Published February 2017
v. 1.0

Printed in the United States of America

CHEESECAKE BOYS

AN ADULT COLORING BOOK

PAUL RICHMOND

DREAMSPINNER PRESS